AROUND THE WORLD
WORLD
IN EIGHTY DAYS

— Jules Verne —

AROUND THE WORLD IN EIGHTY DAYS

PETER HADDOCK PUBLISHING

Published in this edition 1997 by Peter Haddock Publishing,
United Kingdom
Reprinted 1999, 2004

© 1997 This arrangement, text and illustrations,
Geddes & Grosset, David Dale House,
New Lanark, Scotland

© Original text John Kennett

Illustrated by Jane Swift (Simon Girling Associates)

ISBN 0 7105 0941 3

Printed and bound in Poland

Contents

To the Reader

I am sure you will have seen a film, or watched a programme on TV, that has been made from some famous book. If you enjoyed the film or programme, you may have decided to read the book.

Then what happens? You get the book and, it's more than likely, you get a shock as well! You turn ten or twenty pages, and nothing seems to *happen*. Where are all the lively people and exciting incidents? When, you say, will the author get down to telling the story? In the end you will probably throw the book aside and give it up. Now, why is that?

Well, perhaps the author was writing for adults and not for children. Perhaps the book was written a long time ago, when people had more time for reading and liked nothing better than a book that would keep them entertained for weeks.

We think differently today. That's why I've taken some of these wonderful books, and retold them for you. If you enjoy them in this shorter form, then I hope that when you are older you will go back to the original books, and enjoy all the more the wonderful stories they have to tell.

About the Author

Jules Verne, born in Nantes in 1828, is still one of the world's most popular authors. He practised law for some years before he published his first adventure story in Paris in 1862. From that time he wrote almost at the rate of a novel a year until his death in 1905. It has been said that his books are dreams come true, because he described in them the wonders of modern invention—such as submarines, aeroplanes, and television—long before they became realities.

Chapter One
Master and Servant

In which Phileas Fogg and Passepartout accept the positions of master and servant respectively.

In the year 1872 the house, No. 7, Savile Row, Burlington Gardens, in which Sheridan died in 1816, was occupied by Phileas Fogg, Esquire, one of the most remarkable members of the Reform Club, though he always appeared very anxious to avoid attention.

Phileas Fogg had succeeded to the house of one of the greatest of English orators; but, unlike his predecessor, no one knew anything of Fogg; he was an enigmatical personage, though brave, and moving in the highest circles. It was said that he resembled Byron, merely in features, for his morals were irreproachable, but he was a Byron with moustaches and beard—an impassive Byron, one who might live a thousand years without getting old.

Though perhaps not a Londoner, Phileas Fogg was English to the backbone. He was never seen on the Stock Exchange, nor at the Bank, nor in any City house. No vessel consigned to Phileas Fogg ever entered the London Docks; he held no position under Government; he was not a lawyer at any of the Inns; he had never pleaded at the Queen's Bench, the Chancery Bar, the Exchequer, nor the Ecclesiastical

Courts; he was not a manufacturer, nor a merchant, nor a farmer; he was not a member of any of the learned societies of the metropolis. He was simply a member of the Reform Club.

If any one asked how he had become a member of such a distinguished club, he was told that he had been proposed by the Barings, who kept his account, which always showed a good balance, and his cheques were regularly honoured.

Was Phileas Fogg rich? Not a doubt of it. But not even the best informed could say how he had made his money, and Fogg was the last person in the world from whom the information could be obtained. He was never extravagant, but not stingy, for whenever his assistance was required for some useful or praiseworthy project he gave willingly and anonymously.

In short, he was one of the most taciturn of men; he spoke as seldom as possible, and appeared more mysterious as a result of his silence. Nevertheless his life was sufficiently open, but it was so mathematically arranged that to the imagination of the curious this circumstance rendered it more suspicious.

Had he travelled? Very likely, for no one knew more about geography than he did. There was no corner of the earth that he didn't know. Sometimes in a few brief sentences he would clear up the rumours in his club respecting some lost or almost forgotten travellers; he would indicate the probabilities, and it would almost seem as if he possessed

the gift of second-sight, so correctly were his anticipations subsequently justified. He must have been everywhere, in spirit at least.

However, one thing was quite certain. He had not been away from London for years. His most intimate acquaintance could declare that he had never been seen anywhere else but at his club, or on his way to and from it. His only amusement was a game of whist or reading the newspapers. At whist, which suited his taciturn disposition, he was generally a winner, but he always spent his winnings in charity. Besides, it is worth notice that he always played for the game, not for the sake of making money. He played as a trial of skill, a fight against difficulties, but a contest in which no exertion was entailed upon him; he had not to move about nor to tire himself, and this suited him thoroughly.

No one knew whether Fogg had a wife or children, or whether he had relations or intimate friends, which are rare enough in all conscience. He lived alone in Savile Row, and no one ever called. He only kept one servant, he breakfasted and dined at his club at regular hours, at the same table, but he never asked an acquaintance to join him, nor did he ever invite a stranger; he went home to bed at midnight exactly, and he never occupied one of the comfortable bedrooms at the Reform. Of the twenty-four hours in each day he spent ten at his own house. If he took exercise it was in the hall at the club, with its mosaic pavement, or in the circular gallery, supported by twenty Ionic

columns. Here he would walk up and down. When he dined or breakfasted, all the cooks, the steward, and the resources of the club were exercised to provide everything he desired. He was waited upon by grave servants dressed in black, who walked softly as they served him upon a special porcelain set, and with the most expensive damask. His sherry was handed to him in priceless decanters precisely cooled, and the port and claret were of the finest vintages.

If life under such conditions be any proof of eccentricity, it must be confessed that eccentricity has its good side.

The house in Savile Row, though not luxurious, was very comfortable; besides, in accordance with the habits of the owner, the service was reduced as much as possible, but Phileas Fogg was most particular - as regards punctuality. On the very day we are introduced to him (the 2nd of October), he had given his servant, James Foster, notice because he had had the temerity to bring up his master's shaving-water at a temperature of 84° instead of 86°, and Phileas was now waiting a successor, who was expected between eleven and half-past eleven o'clock.

Phileas Fogg was seated in his armchair, his feet at "attention," his hands resting on his knees, his body upright, and his head erect. He was watching the clock. This complex piece of machinery told the hours, minutes, seconds, the days of the week, month, and year. When the chime of half-past eleven rang out, Mr. Fogg would leave the house for his club.

Just then a knock was heard at the door of the little sitting-room, and James Foster appeared.

"The new valet has come, sir," he said.

A young fellow of about thirty entered, and bowed to Mr. Fogg.

"You are a Frenchman, and your name is John?" said Mr. Fogg.

"Jean, if it is all the same to you, sir," replied the newcomer—"Jean Passepartout—a name which will stick to me, and which will be justified by my natural aptitude for change. I believe I am honest; but, to tell the truth, I have tried a great many things. I have been a singer, a circus-rider, an acrobat, and a rope-walker, then I became a professor of gymnastics, and at last, to make myself useful, I enrolled myself as a fireman in Paris, and can show you the scars of several burns. But it is now five years since I left France, and as I wished to enjoy domestic life I became a valet in England. Now being without a situation, and having heard that Mr. Phileas Fogg was the most punctual and the most sedentary gentleman in the United Kingdom, I have taken the liberty to come here for a quiet life, and to forget my name of Passepartout."

"Passepartout suits me," replied Mr. Fogg. "You have been recommended to me. You know my conditions?"

"Yes, sir."

"Well, what time do you make it?"

"Twenty-two minutes past eleven," replied Passepartout, pulling out an enormous silver watch.

"You are slow," said Mr. Fogg.

"Excuse me, sir, that is impossible."

"You are four minutes behind time. Never mind it is sufficient to have made a note of it. Well, then, from this moment, twenty-nine minutes past eleven a.m., the 2nd of October, 1872, you are in my service."

As he spoke, Mr. Fogg rose, took up his hat in his left hand, put it on his head automatically, and left the room without another word.

Passepartout heard the door shut once—that was his master going out; he heard it shut a second time—that was his predecessor, James Foster, who was leaving in his turn.

Passepartout was left alone in the house in Savile Row.

Chapter Two

Passepartout's New Home

"My goodness," said Passepartout, "I have seen figures at Madame Tussaud's quite as cheerful as my new master."

It should be said that Madame Tussaud's figures are made of wax, and want nothing but the power of speech.

During the short time that Passepartout had been in the company of Mr. Fogg he had scrutinized him carefully. His future master seemed to be about forty, tall and well made, not too stout, and with noble, handsome features. His hair was fair, his brow was open, his face rather pale, and he had beautiful teeth.

He appeared to possess a very cool and collected disposition—common to all those who prefer deeds to words. Calm, phlegmatic, with clear steady eyes, he was very much a type of those Englishmen whom one frequently meets. In his everyday life Mr. Fogg gave one the idea of a perfectly-balanced being—a sort of chronometer—in fact, he was punctuality personified, and so much could be seen in the "expression of his hands and feet," for with men, as amongst the lower animals, the limbs are expressive of passions.

Phileas Fogg was one of those people who are never in a hurry, and being always ready are economical of their

movements. He never took a step too much; he always went the shortest way. He never wasted a look at the ceiling, and never permitted himself a needless gesture. No one had ever seen him agitated or annoyed; he never hurried himself, but was always in time.

He lived alone, and, so to speak, outside the social scale; he knew that there was a great deal of friction in life, and as friction retards progress he never rubbed against any one.

As for Passepartout, he was a Parisian of Parisians. For five years he had lived in England as *valet-de-chambre*, during which time he had vainly sought for such a master as he had now engaged himself to.

Passepartout was a good fellow, with pleasant features, ruddy lips ready to kiss or to eat, a good-natured serviceable lad, possessing one of those round heads which one is so glad to see on the shoulders of one's friends.

He had blue eyes; his face was somewhat stout; he was very strong and muscular. He wore his brown hair in rather a ragged fashion.

If sculptors of antiquity knew eighteen ways of arranging the hair of Minerva, Passepartout knew only one way of arranging his—three strokes of a comb was sufficient for him.

To say that the young man's character would agree with Mr. Fogg's would be rash; whether Passepartout would suit his master remained to be proved—time will tell. After having passed his youth in such a vagabond fashion the

lad looked forward to some response. He had often heard of the English methodical way of living, but up to the present time he had not succeeded in finding it. He had "taken root" nowhere, and he had tried six situations—in each there was something which did not suit him.

His latest proprietor, young Lord Longsferry, M.P., had passed his nights in questionable society, and had ended by being carried home by policemen. Passepartout, who wished above all things to respect his master, remonstrated. His suggestion was taken in ill part, and he discharged himself.

Just then he heard that Phileas Fogg was in want of a valet, and offered himself for the situation. A person whose existence was so methodical, who never slept away from home, who never travelled, who was never away for a day, was the very master for him. He presented himself and was successful, as we already know.

So Passepartout, at half-past eleven o'clock, found himself alone in the house. He immediately started to look around, and explored the house from cellar to garret. He was very pleased; the house seemed like a very pretty snail-shell, but a shell warmed and lighted. Passepartout soon found his room on the second floor, and was quite satisfied with it. Electric bells and acoustic tubes put him in communication with the rooms below. On the chimney-piece was an electric clock corresponding exactly with that in Mr. Fogg's bedroom—the pendulums beat time to a second.

"This will do," said Passepartout to himself.

He observed also in his room that a notice was fixed above the clock; this was a programme of his daily service from eight in the morning, when Mr. Fogg got up, till half-past eleven, when he went down to his club. It included all details: the tea and toast at twenty-three minutes past eight, the shaving-water at thirty-seven minutes past nine, his attendance on his master at twenty minutes to ten, etc. Then from half-past eleven a.m. till midnight, when this methodical gentleman went to bed, everything was provided for. Passepartout was delighted, and joyfully sat down to master the details of the programme.

His master's wardrobe was well stocked and marvellously neat. Every article bore a number and was noted in a book which showed at what seasons certain suits were to be worn. The same regulations were applied to boots and shoes.

In fact, in this house in Savile Row, which had been the temple of disorder in the days of Sheridan, order now reigned supreme. There was no library and there were no books; but these would have been useless to Mr. Fogg, as there was a capital library and a reading-room at his club. In his bedroom was a safe both burglar-proof and fireproof. There were no firearms in the house, nor any weapon of war or for sport. Everything denoted that the occupant was a man of most pacific character.

After having examined everything in detail, Passepartout rubbed his hands; his round face beamed with joy as he said—

"This will do for me very nicely. We understand each other thoroughly, Mr. Fogg and I. He is a most domestic individual—a perfect machine. Well, I am not sorry to serve a machine after all."

Chapter Three

A Robbery and a Bet

Phileas Fogg left his house at half-past eleven,

And having placed his right foot before his left five hundred and seventy-five times, and his left foot before his right five hundred and seventy-six times, he reached the Reform Club. He immediately went to the breakfast-room and took his place at the usual table near one of the open windows. His breakfast consisted of one *hors d'oeuvre*, a piece of boiled fish, a slice of underdone beef with mushrooms, rhubarb and gooseberry tart, and some Cheshire cheese, the whole washed down with some excellent tea, which is a speciality of the Reform Club.

At forty-seven minutes past twelve he went into the sitting-room, a magnificent apartment hung with splendid pictures. A servant handed him an uncut copy of the *Times*, which Fogg himself cut and folded with long practiced dexterity. The perusal of this paper occupied him until forty-five minutes past three, and the *Standard*, which succeeded, lasted till dinner, which was eaten under similar conditions to his breakfast.

At twenty minutes to six he returned to the drawing-room and read the *Morning Chronicle*.

Half-an-hour later several members of the club came in

and stood with their backs to the fire. These were Mr. Fogg's usual partners at whist, and were all enthusiastic players. They were Andrew Stuart, the engineer, John Sullivan and Samuel Fallentin, bankers, Thomas Flanagan, a brewer, and Gauthier Ralph, one of the directors of the Bank of England, all men of wealth and standing, even in that club which includes so many members of consequence in financial and business circles.

"Well, Ralph," said Flanagan, "how about this robber?"

"Oh," said Stuart, "the Bank will lose the money."

"I expect not," said Ralph. "I fancy we shall be able to catch the thief. There are very clever detectives at all the principal ports in Europe and America, and the fellow will find it difficult to escape."

"They have the description of the thief, I suppose?" said Stuart.

"In the first place he is not a thief at all," replied Ralph seriously.

"What! Do not you call a man a robber who has made away with fifty-five thousand pounds in banknotes?"

"No," replied Gauthier Ralph.

"He is a man of business, then," said John Sullivan.

"The *Morning Chronicle* says he is a gentleman."

This observation was made by Phileas Fogg, who rose up from the sea of paper surrounding him, and greeted his group of friends.

The subject of discussion, which all the papers of the kingdom had taken up, was a certain robbery which had

been committed three days before—namely, on the 29th of September. A pile of bank-notes to the amount of fifty-five thousand pounds had been stolen from the counter at the Bank of England.

What astonished everybody was the fact that the theft had been so easily managed, and Gauthier Ralph took the trouble to explain that when the fifty-five thousand pounds were stolen, the cashier was industriously entering a sum of three shillings and sixpence, and of course could not have his eyes everywhere.

It may be remarked in passing, and this may account for the robbery, that the Bank of England has great faith in the honesty of the public. There are no guards nor commissionaires, or gratings; gold, silver, and notes are freely exposed, and, so to speak, at the mercy of anyone. No one is suspected. One of the closest observers of British customs has related the following experience:—

One day he was in the Bank parlour, and had the curiosity to examine an ingot of gold weighing six or seven pounds which happened to be on the table. He picked up the nugget, and when he had satisfied his curiosity he passed it to his neighbour. He in his turn passed it to the next man, and so on; the nugget went from hand to hand to the end of a long corridor, and was not returned to its place for half-an-hour, and all the time the cashier never even as much as looked up.

But on the 29th of September matters did not go so smoothly. The package of bank-notes was not returned,

and when the clock in the "drawing office" struck five, at which hour the Bank is closed, fifty-five thousand pounds was written off to profit and loss.

As soon as the robbery was ascertained to be a fact, the most able detectives were sent down to Liverpool, Glasgow, Havre, to Suez, to Brindisi, and New York, etc., with a promise of a reward (if successful) of two thousand pounds, and five per cent. on the amount recovered. In the meantime these detectives were directed to take particular notice of all travellers arriving at or departing from these ports.

Now, as the *Morning Chronicle* said, there was some reason to think that the thief was not a member of a gang at all. More than once on the 29th of September a gentlemanly, well-dressed man had been seen frequently in the Bank near the place where the robbery had been committed. An exact description of this gentleman had been provided to all the detectives, and so some hopeful people, amongst whom was Gauthier Ralph, believed that the thief could not possibly escape.

Of course the robbery was the chief topic of conversation everywhere. The probabilities of success were discussed, and it is not surprising that the members of the Reform Club were also interested, particularly as one of the deputy governors of the Bank belonged to the club.

Mr. Ralph had no doubt of the ultimate success of the search because of the reward offered, which would stimulate the brains of the detectives, but his friend Andrew

Stuart was of a different opinion. The discussion between these gentlemen was continued even at the whist-table, where Stuart was Flanagan's partner, and Fallentin played with Phileas Fogg. They did not argue while they played, but between the rubbers conversation flowed.

"I maintain that the odds are in favour of the thief," said Stuart. "He must be a sharp fellow."

"But," replied Ralph, "where can he go to?"

"What do you say?"

"Where can he go to?"

"I don't know," replied Stuart, "but there are plenty of places in the world for him."

"There used to be," said Phileas Fogg in an undertone. "Will you cut, please? "he added, passing the cards to Flanagan.

The conversation ceased for the moment, but Andrew Stuart took it up again by saying—

"Used to be! What do you mean by that? Has the world grown smaller by any chance?"

"Of course it has," replied Ralph. "I agree with Mr. Fogg the world has grown smaller, because you can go round it ten times more quickly than you could a hundred years ago; so the search for a thief will be more rapid."

"And make the escape of the thief easier also."

"Your lead, Mr. Stuart," said Phileas Fogg.

But the incredulous Stuart would not be convinced, and when the "hand" was finished he continued.

"It must be confessed, Mr. Ralph," he said, "that you

have discovered that in one sense the world has grown smaller, because you can go round it in three months."

"In eighty days," said Phileas Fogg.

"That is right gentlemen," added John Sullivan, "for, since the opening of the Great Indian Peninsular Railway between Rothal and Allahabad it can be done in that time. Here is the estimate given by the *Morning Chronicle*:—

"'From London to Suez by Mont Cenis
and Brindisi. Rail and Steamer .... 7 days
From Suez to Bombay. Steamer 13
From Bombay to Calcutta. Railway .... 3 days
From Calcutta to Hong-Kong. Steamer .... 13 days
From Hong-Kong to Yokohama. Steamer ..... 6 days
From Yokohama to San Francisco Steamer . 22 days
From San Francisco to New York. Railway .... 7 days
From New York to London. Steamer
and Railway .... 9 days.

Total .... 80 days.'"

"Yes, eighty days," cried Stuart, who unfortunately made a misdeal; "but that does not take into consideration bad weather, contrary winds, shipwreck, or railway accident."

"All included," replied Fogg as he continued to play, for this time the discussion did not cease with the deal.

"But suppose Hindoos or Indians take up the rail, stop the trains, pillage the baggage, and scalp the travellers?"

"All included," returned Fogg quietly. "Two by honours," he added.

Stuart, who was "pony," took up the cards and said—

"In theory, no doubt, you are right, Mr. Fogg, but in practice—"

"In practice too, Mr. Stuart."

"I should like to see you do it."

"It rests with you. Suppose we go together?"

"Heaven forbid!" exclaimed Stuart, "but I will bet you four thousand pounds that the thing is impossible in the time."

"On the contrary, it is quite possible," replied Mr. Fogg.

"Well, then, do it."

"Go round the world in eighty days?"

"Yes."

"I will."

"When?"

"At once."

"Ah! that is all nonsense," exclaimed Stuart, who was beginning to be vexed at his partner's insistence. "Let us continue the game."

"You must deal, then," replied Fogg; "the last is a misdeal."

Andrew Stuart took up the cards in an uncertain manner, and put them down again.

"Well, then, Mr. Fogg," he said, "I will bet you four thousand pounds "

"My dear, Stuart," said Fallentin, "don't be absurd. He is not serious."

"When I say I bet," replied Andrew Stuart, "I am quite serious."

"All right," said Mr. Fogg; then, turning to his friends, he said—

"I have twenty thousand pounds deposited with Baring Brothers. I will willingly risk that sum."

"Twenty thousand pounds!" exclaimed John Sullivan. "You might lose it all by some unforeseen accident."

"The unforeseen does not exist," replied Phileas Fogg simply.

"But, Mr. Fogg, this eighty days is but the minimum of time."

"A minimum well employed is sufficient."

"But in order not to exceed it you must pass with mathematical certainty from railways to steamers, and from steamers to railways."

"I will be accurate."

"After all, this can be but a joke."

"A true Briton never jokes when he has a bet depending on a subject. I bet you twenty thousand pounds that I will go round the world in eighty days or less—that is to say, in nineteen hundred and twenty hours, or a hundred and fifteen thousand two hundred minutes. Will you take it?"

"Yes," replied the others after consultation.

"Very well, then," replied Mr. Fogg; "the Continental Mail starts at 8.45, and we will go by it."

"This evening!" exclaimed Stuart.

"This evening," replied Fogg. Then looking at a pocket

almanac, he continued, "This is Wednesday the 2nd of October; I shall be in London in this room on Saturday evening the 21st of December, at a quarter before nine p.m.; if not the twenty thousand pounds at Barings' will be yours. Here is my cheque for that sum."

A memorandum to this effect was written out and signed on the spot. Phileas Fogg was perfectly cool. He had certainly not bet to win the money, and he had only staked £20,000, half of his fortune, because he knew he might have to spend the other amount in carrying out his almost impossible project. His adversaries were quite excited, not because of the magnitude of the stake, but because they had scruples about betting at all under such conditions.

Seven o'clock struck, and they suggested that Mr. Fogg should go home and prepare for his journey.

"I am always ready," replied that cool gentleman as he continued to deal. "Diamonds are trumps, Mr. Stuart; it is your lead."

Chapter Four

The Journey Begins

Phileas Fogg left the Reform Club at twenty-five minutes past seven. At ten minutes to eight, he opened the door of his house and entered. He went to his bedroom and called loudly, "Passepartout!"

Passepartout was seated in his room pondering on his future with Phileas Fogg, sure that he had found exactly the type of master he liked—a home-loving man, who *never* travelled.

Passepartout had spent his life travelling. He had enjoyed his various careers as a travelling singer, a circus rider, a gymnast and a fireman in Paris. He had made the correct decsion to become a man-servant in England, but all his employers had been restless and always dashing from one place to another—which did not suit Passepartout at all.

Phileas, however, suited him perfectly. His life was planned and time-tabled, from eight in the morning until midnight. Passepartout had never known such peace. Until this moment.

. . . Passepartout could not believe that his master had called. It was not the right hour.

"Passepartout!" Mr. Fogg called again, without raising his voice much.

Passepartout presented himself.

"We leave in ten minutes for Dover and Calais," said Phileas.

Passepartout blew out his cheeks and pulled a face. His eyes popped out of his head a little.

"Monsieur is going to leave home?" he asked.

"Yes. We are going to travel all the way round the world."

Passepartout's eyes opened wide, his eyebrows shot up, he threw up his hands. "Around the world!" he murmured, and his eyes seemed to revolve in his head.

"In eighty days," replied Mr. Fogg, "so we have not a moment to lose."

"But the trunks?" cried Passepartout.

"Not wanted. Only a carpet-bag. In it two woollen shirts, and three pairs of socks. The same for you. We will buy anything else we want on the way. Go."

Passepartout went, shaking his head. Had his master gone mad? No. It must be a joke.

By eight o'clock, Passepartout rejoined his master, his carpet-bag packed. Mr. Fogg was ready. He took the bag, opened it, and slipped into it a heavy package of those fine bank-notes which are currency in all countries.

"Take this bag, and look after it. There are twenty thousand pounds in it, "he said.

The bag nearly slipped out of Passepartout's hands, as if the money had been in gold, and weighed very heavily.

At twenty minutes past eight a carriage put them down at the gate of Charing Cross Station. Phileas ordered

Passepartout to get two first-class tickets for Paris. The five gentlemen with whom Phileas had laid his bet were waiting.

"Well, gentlemen," he said, "I am going, as you see. The various stamps put upon my passport will help you check my journey, and you will see me again in exactly eighty days. Saturday, December 21st, at a quarter before nine p.m., in the saloon of the Reform Club. Until then, gentlemen—"

At eighty forty-five the whistle sounded, and the train started. A fine rain was falling. Phileas leaned back in his corner and did not speak. Passepartout hugged the carpet-bag. Suddenly he gave a cry of despair.

"What is the matter?" asked Mr. Fogg.

"Parbleu! I forgot to turn off the gas burner in my room."

"Very well," replied Mr. Fogg coldly, it will burn for eighty days at your expense!"

Chapter Five

The Detective

News of Phileas Fogg's wager reached the papers. A great deal was written about his "tour of the world" and everyone took sides for or against him. Most people declared that he must be mad, as the possibility of accidents or bad weather, leading to a delay of even one day, was so great that he was almost certain to ruin himself.

His photograph was published in the *London Illustrated News,* where it attracted the notice of certain members of the police at Scotland Yard, and was carefully examined. It matched perfectly the description of the distinguished and well-dressed gentleman who had been seen in the paying room of the bank. The police discovered how mysterious Phileas Fogg's life had been; his isolation and his sudden departure. It became clear that this person, under the pretext of a journey round the world, supported by a senseless bet, had no other aim than to mislead the agents of the English police. The newspapers published these suspicions; the honourable gentleman disappeared to make room for the bank robber.

The telegraph wires buzzed and hummed as the description was sent out to many places. One of these places was Suez, where, on Wednesday, October 9th, there was

expected at eleven a.m., the steamer *Mongolia,* which made regular trips from Brindisi to Bombay by the Suez Canal.

On the wharf at Suez, awaiting the arrival of the ship, was a small, spare man with the swift movements and sharp features of a bird. His name was Fix, and he was a detective set to watch all travellers taking the Suez route. Two days before, he had received from the Commissioner of the Metropolitan Police a description of the supposed bank-robber.

Eleven o'clock was striking when the ship came to anchor by the wharf. In a little while, many of the passengers began coming ashore in boats which had gone out to hail the ship.

Fix was studying all who landed, when one of them approached him and asked for the office of the English consular agent. As he spoke, he held out a passport. Fix took it, and read the description on it. He gave a start. His mouth went tight under the beaked nose. The description matched the one he had received from London.

"This passport isn't yours," he said to the passenger.

"No," replied Passepartout. "It is my master's. He is staying on board."

"He must come ashore," said the detective firmly, "to establish his identity at the Consul's office. It is essential."

"And where is the office?"

"There at the corner of the square," replied the detective, pointing out a house two hundred paces off.

"Then I will tell my master. Thank you for your help."

Passepartout bowed to Fix, and returned aboard the steamer.

The detective left the wharf and turned quickly towards the Consul's office. Within two or three minutes, he had told the Consul of his suspicions.

"And he is coming to have his passport stamped?" asked the Consul.

"Yes. I hope you will refuse to do so."

"I have no right to do that, if all is in order."

"But I must delay this man until I have received a warrant of arrest from London."

"Mr. Fix, that is your business," replied the Consul. "I have nothing to do with arrests."

Soon Phileas and Passepartout arrived. Phileas presented his passport, and asked the Consul to stamp it. The Consul examined the passport carefully, while Fix, from a corner of the room, devoured the stranger with his eyes.

"You are Phileas Fogg," asked the Consul, "and you come from London?"

"Yes."

"And you are going—?"

"To Bombay. I wish, however, to prove by your stamp that I have visited Suez."

"Very well, sir."

The Consul signed and dated the passport. Mr. Fogg settled the fee, bowed, and went out, followed by his servant.

"He looks to me, Mr Fix," said the Consul, "like a perfectly honest man."

"Possibly," replied Fix coldly. "He also resembles, feature for feature, the robber whose description I have received."

"You know that descriptions may be misleading."

"I am sure of this one," replied Fix. "And he shall not escape me!" and he marched out of the office.

In the meantime, Mr. Fogg had gone back to the wharf. There he gave some orders to his servant, then got into a boat and returned to the ship, leaving Passepartout behind. Fix approached him.

"Well, my friend," he said, "are you enjoying your trip?"

"Yes indeed, monsieur," replied Passepartout, "but we go so quickly that I have no time to see anything. Just now I wish to buy some articles, but I must take care not to miss the steamer."

"You have time enough," replied Fix. "It is only noon!"

Passepartout pulled out his large watch.

"Noon? Pshaw! It is eight minutes to ten!"

"Your watch is slow," replied Fix.

"My watch is *never* slow! A family watch that has come down from my great-grandfather!"

"I think I know what is wrong," replied Fix. "You have kept London time, which is about two hours slower than Suez. You must be careful to set your watch at noon in each country."

"What! I, touch my watch!" cried Passepartout. "Never!"

"Well, then, it will not agree with the sun."

"So much the worse for the sun, monsieur! The sun will

be wrong, then!" and he put his watch back into his fob with a magnificent gesture.

As they went along, Passepartout talked eagerly to this good-hearted stranger and told the whole story of this master's bet. The detective's suspicions were heightened. This large sum carried away, this haste to arrive in distant countries! He kept the Frenchman talking; learned that he did not know his master well; that he lived alone in London, was a mysterious man, and all the rest of it.

"The deuce!" said Passepartout of a sudden. "There is one thing that bothers me it is my burner."

"What burner?"

"My gas-burner, which I forgot to turn off, and which is burning at my expense."

Fix was no longer listening. They had reached the shops, and he left the Frenchman there to make his purchases. He returned in great haste to the telegraph office, and sent off a dispatch in the following words:

"SUEZ TO LONDON

"Rowan, Commissioner of Police, Central Office, Scotland Yard: I have traced the bank robber, Phileas Fogg. Send warrant of arrest at once to Bombay.

"FIX, *Detective.*"

A half-hour later, Fix, with his light baggage in his hand, and well supplied with money, went on board the *Mongolia*. Soon afterwards the steamer was threading its way through the Red Sea, bound for Aden and Bombay.

Chapter Six

The End of the Line

The distance between Suez and Aden is exactly thirteen hundred and ten miles. The *Mongolia,* whose engineer had been promised a splendid reward by Phileas Fogg if the ship reached Bombay ahead of time, had her fires well kept up, and sped along rapidly.

Mr. Fogg had in his cabin a memorandum-book, arranged in columns, which indicated, from the 2nd of October to the 21st of December—the month, the day of the week, and the time-tabled and actual arrivals at each principal point, which allowed him to figure the gain made or the loss experienced at each place on the route. He knew always whether he was ahead of time or behind.

As for Passepartout, on the day after leaving Suez, he was pleased to meet on deck the man who had been so much help to him at Suez.

"Delighted to meet you again, Monsieur—?" - "Fix."

"Are you going to Bombay, too?"

"Yes," replied Fix. "I am an agent of the Peninsular Company."

After this meeting, Passepartout and the detective talked often together.

In the meantime, the steamer positively sped along. On

the evening of the 14th, she put into the harbour at Aden. There she was to lay in coal, and would be four hours doing it, but had gained fifteen hours on the trip down the Red Sea.

Mr. Fogg and his servant landed, to have Fogg's passport stamped. Fix followed them without being noticed, until they returned on board.

At six that evening the *Mongolia* steamed out into the Indian Ocean. She had one hundred and sixty-eight hours to cover the distance between Aden and Bombay. All was favourable; the wind kept in the north-west, and the sails came to the aid of the steam.

On Sunday, the 20th of October, towards noon, they sighted the Indian coast. The steamer entered the harbour, and at half-past four she put in at the wharves of Bombay. She was not, in fact, due there until October 22nd. This was a gain of two days, since his departure from London, and Phileas Fogg noted it down in his memorandum-book.

So far, so good. Now for the journey across India by the newly-opened railway, which put Bombay at only three days from Calcutta.

The train left at eight o'clock that night. Mr. Fogg gave his servant directions for some purchases, warned him to be at the station before eight, and then turned his steps towards the passport office. After that, he went to the station and there had dinner served.

Detective Fix had also landed from the *Mongolia* and

hurried to the office of the Commissioner of Police in Bombay. He made himself known; asked if a warrant of arrest had arrived from London. It had not.

While this was going on, Passepartout was wandering through the streets of Bombay. He was passing the magnificent Hindu temple on Malebar Hill, when he took it into his head to go inside. He was ignorant of two things: that entrance to certain Hindu temples is forbidden, and that the believers themselves cannot enter without leaving their shoes at the door. The British Government in India punishes severely all who violate these rules.

Passepartout went in, like a simple traveller, and was admiring the ornamentation when he was suddenly seized and thrown down upon the floor. Three priests, with furious looks, rushed upon him, tore off his shoes and stockings, and started to beat him, uttering savage cries. The Frenchman, vigorous and agile, rose again quickly; felled two of his attackers, and rushed from the temple. By mingling with the crowd, he soon out-distanced the third Hindu, who had followed him.

At five minutes to eight, breathless, hatless, and barefoot, he came to the station. Fix, who had gone there to keep an eye on Phileas, was standing close by in a dark place, and heard the Frenchman tell his adventure in a few words to his master.

"I hope it won't happen to you again," was all Phileas said, and then the two took their seats in the train.

"I'll stay here," Fix said to himself, in great satisfaction.

"A crime committed upon Indian soil! I have my man!" A moment or two later, the locomotive gave a loud whistle, and the train disappeared into the darkness.

Passepartout was in the same compartment as his master. A third traveller sat in the opposite corner, one of the acquaintances made by Mr. Fogg during the trip from Suez to Bombay: a brigadier-general, Sir Francis Cromarty, who was rejoining his troops at Benares. The General knew all about Phileas' bet, and his plan for a tour of the world. Now Phileas told him of Passepartout's adventure in the Hindu temple, while Passepartout slept soundly, his feet wrapped up in his cloak.

"The British Government frowns upon this kind of trespass," Sir Francis said. "It insists, and rightly, that the religious customs of the Hindus should be respected. If your servant had been taken—"

"He would have been sentenced and punished," said Mr. Fogg. "Fortunately, he escaped."

They let the matter drop, and both were soon asleep. All through the night the train sped on its way, over vast plains and through immense stretches of jungle.

Just after noon, next day, it stopped at Burhampoor, and Passepartout was able to buy a pair of ornamented slippers to cover his bare feet. Now that they were hurrying across India, his mind had undergone a change. All at once, he was very much on his master's side, and disturbed at the thought of delays, the possible accidents which might occur upon the route. He wanted Phileas to win his bet,

and trembled at the thought that he might have ruined everything the evening before by his unpardonable foolishness. He cursed the stopping of the train, and worried about the passing of the time.

The next day, the 22nd of October, Passepartout, having looked at his watch, replied to a question of Sir Francis Cromarty's that it was three o'clock in the morning. His watch, still regulated by the meridian of Greenwich, was, in fact, four hours slow. Sir Francis tried to make him understand that he ought to regulate his watch on each new meridian; that since he was all the time moving towards the east, in the face of the sun, the days were shorter by as many times four minutes as he had crossed degrees. It was useless. Passepartout kept his watch at London Time.

At eight o'clock in the morning, the train stopped on the edge of a big clearing, in which were some bungalows and workmen's huts. The conductor passed along the train calling out: "All passengers will get out here!"

Mr. Fogg looked at Sir Francis Cromarty, who was obviously puzzled by this stop in the middle of a forest. Passepartout jumped down on to the track, vanished for a minute or two, and returned, crying: "Monsieur, no more railway!"

"What do you mean?" asked Sir Francis.

"I mean that the train goes no farther. The line has come to an end!"

Chapter Seven

A Ride on an Elephant

Sir Francis puffed and blew out his cheeks, and got down from the car in a very agitated state. Phileas Fogg, in no hurry, followed him.

"Where are we?" Sir Francis asked the conductor.

"At the village of Kholby."

"We stop here?"

"We must. The railway is not finished. There is still a section of fifty miles to build between this point and Allahabad, where the track begins again."

"But you give tickets from Bombay to Calcutta," exploded the indignant General.

"Of course," replied the conductor, "But travellers know very well that they must make their own way from Kholby to Allahabad."

"Sir Francis," said Mr. Fogg simply, "let us look for some means of getting to Allahabad."

"Mr. Fogg, this delay will ruin you—"

"Not at all. I have gained two days which I can afford to lose. A steamer leaves Calcutta for Hong-Kong at noon on the 25th. This is only the 23rd, and we shall reach Calcutta in time."

Mr. Fogg, Sir Francis, and Passepartout agreed to hunt

separately through the village for a means of transport. Phileas and the General returned without having found anything faster than broken-down ox-carts.

Passepartout, who had just come up, said, "Monsieur, I believe I have found a means of conveyance—an elephant, in fact, monsieur, belonging to an Indian who lives close by."

They went and saw the elephant, which his owner called Kiouni, and Phileas Fogg determined to employ him. When, however, he asked the Indian if he would hire him his elephant the man flatly refused. Fogg offered ten pounds an hour. Refused. Twenty pounds. Still refused. Forty pounds. Refused again. The Indian would not be tempted. Phileas Fogg then offered to buy the animal for one thousand pounds. The Indian would not sell!

Sir Francis begged Phileas to reflect. Mr. Fogg replied that a bet of twenty thousand pounds was at stake, that this elephant was necessary to him, and that, should he pay twenty times his value, he meant to have him!

He went again for the Indian, whose small eyes lit up with greed, showing that it was only a question of price. Phileas offered twelve hundred, fifteen hundred, eighteen hundred, and finally two thousand pounds. Sir Francis had gone purple in the face, and Passepartout had turned pale. The Indian accepted two thousand.

All that remained was to find a guide. A young Parsee, with an intelligent face, offered his services. Mr. Fogg accepted him, and promised him a large reward to sharpen

his wits. The elephant was covered with a saddlecloth, and a howdah was strapped to each flank.

Phileas paid the Indian in bank-notes taken from the famous carpet-bag, then offered to convey Sir Francis to Allahabad. The General accepted; one more passenger was not likely to tire this enormous animal. Some provisions were bought; Sir Francis took his seat in one howdah, Phileas in the other. Passepartout got astride the animal, between his master and the General. The Parsee perched upon the elephant's neck, and off they went at a rough trot.

For some hours they moved through jungle country, then came out of the forest to cross a huge plain, bristling with scanty shrubs, and strewn with large boulders.

At two o'clock, when they were some twelve miles from Allahabad, they moved into jungle again. After some time the elephant, showing signs of uneasiness, came to a halt.

"What is the matter?" asked Sir Francis.

"I do not know," replied the Parsee, listening to a confused murmur which they now heard.

In a minute or two the noise became recognizable as the sound of human voices and brass instruments. The Parsee jumped down, fastened the elephant to a tree, and plunged into the undergrowth. He scurried back a few minutes later.

"A Brahmin procession is coming this way!" he cried excitedly. "It will be better if we are not seen!"

He unfastened the elephant and led him into a thicket, telling the others not to descend.

The noise grew closer and louder, a weird chanting mingled with the crash and clash of drums and cymbals. The head of the procession appeared, on a path, only fifty yards away.

It was led by priests in long robes. They were surrounded by men, women, and children, chanting a kind of dirge. Behind them, on a cart drawn by zebus, was a hideous statue; it had four arms, haggard eyes, tangled hair, and a long tongue that hung out between brilliantly coloured lips. Around its neck hung a collar of skulls; around its waist a girdle of human hands.

Behind the cart came some Brahmins in rich costumes, dragging a woman who seemed hardly able to stand. She was young, light of skin, and strikingly beautiful. A gold-embroidered tunic fell from her throat to her knees.

Behind her were guards, armed with swords and long pistols, four of them carrying upon their shoulders a corpse upon a stretcher. The body was that of an old man, dressed in the rich garments of a rajah. He was followed by musicians and a rear-guard of fanatics, whose cries often drowned the noise of the instruments.

Sir Francis looked at all this sadly. He turned to the guide, and said: "A suttee?"

The Parsee nodded, and put a finger to his lips. The procession wound on its way and disappeared among the trees. Its noise faded.

"What," asked Phileas Fogg, "is a suttee?"

"It is the custom in certain parts of India," replied Sir

Francis, "to burn a widow on the funeral pyre of her husband. That young woman you have just seen will be burned tomorrow with the body they were carrying on the stretcher."

"How do these barbarous customs still exist in India?" asked Phileas. "Why have the British not stamped them out?"

"We have—in many parts of India," replied Sir Francis, "but unfortunately we do not have influence over this territory of Bundelcund."

"That unfortunate woman," murmured Passepartout. "Burned alive!"

"Yes," replied the General grimly, "burned! If she were not, she would be treated like an outcast. Her relatives would shave her head, refuse to feed her, and treat her like some unclean creature. These poor women are often driven to choose death because they know, only too well, what would be done to them if they didn't!"

"This lady did not choose to die," said the Parsee, shaking his head. "The priests have drugged her."

"Where are they taking her?"

"To the temple of Pillaji, two miles from here. There she will pass the night, waiting for the sacrifice."

"And this will take place?"

"At first light."

There was a long silence. The guide turned away and led the elephant from the thicket. Mr. Fogg called to him to wait.

"Perhaps we could save this woman."

"Save her, Mr. Fogg!" cried Sir Francis.

"I still have twelve hours to spare. I can devote them to her."

"Why, you are a man of heart!" said Sir Francis, astonished.

"Sometimes," replied Phileas Fogg simply. "When I have time."

Chapter Eight
The Rescue

Passepartout and Sir Francis were willing to risk the rescue, but what of their guide? Would he not side with the Indians? Sir Francis put the question to him frankly.

"Sir," replied the guide, "I am a Parsee, and that woman is a Parsee. Make use of me, please. But I must tell you that we risk not only our lives, but horrible punishments if we are taken."

"Indeed," said Phileas calmly, "then we must try not to be taken. We had best wait for darkness before we act."

The guide then told them what he knew of the victim. She was the daughter of a rich merchant of Bombay. Her name was Aouda, and she had been given an English education. Left an orphan, she had been married against her will to the old Rajah of Bundelcund. Three months later she was a widow. Knowing the fate that waited her, she fled, but was caught, and had been forced by the Rajah's relatives to make this sacrifice, from which it seemed, she could not escape.

"She *shall* escape," murmured Phileas, and it was decided that they should turn the elephant towards the temple of Pillaji, and wait close by until the coming of night.

They halted, half an hour later, under a thick clump of

trees, five hundred yards from the temple. They could hear the yellings of the fanatics. Their guide knew the lay-out of the temple, but as yet they had made no plan.

They ate a rough meal, and waited. When night came down, they followed their guide, creeping under the branches, until they reached the bank of a small river. There, by the light of torches set in iron stands, they saw a great pile of wood; the funeral pyre, made of costly sandal wood, and saturated with perfumed oil. On its upper part lay the embalmed body of the Rajah. A hundred paces from this pile rose the temple, showing pale and white above the trees.

They approached the temple and stopped at the edge of a clearing, lit up by torches. The ground was covered with groups of sleepers; the soldiers of the Rajah were watching at the temple doors, and pacing up and down with drawn swords. The place was surrounded by guards and sleepers. It was clearly impossible for any stranger to enter the place unseen.

"What can we do but leave?" asked the General in a low voice.

"Wait," said Phileas Fogg curtly.

"But what hope is there?"

"The chance which escapes us now may offer itself at the last moment."

Passepartout was perched upon the lower branches of a tree. As he sat there, an idea entered his head. He had been haunted by the picture of the old Rajah, lying there,

cold and dead, upon the funeral pyre. He could not drive
it from his mind, and then, an idea came to him in a flash.
He took a deep breath. It was a chance—perhaps the only
one. He thought no more, but slid down, with the ease of
a snake, along the branch to the ground and glided away
among the trees.

The hours passed. A first faint flush of light touched the
tree-tops. A drum began to beat. The groups wakened up;
chants and cries burst out anew. The hour had come in
which the helpless victim was to die.

The doors of the temple were opened wide. In the light
of torches, the watchers could see the victim, whom two
priests were dragging to the outside. It seemed to them
that the unfortunate woman was trying to escape from
her executioners. Sir Francis's heart throbbed violently.
Phileas was clutching an open pocket-knife, his only
weapon, in his right hand.

Then the young woman seemed to fall back into her
drugged stupor, moving mechanically between the fakirs,
who escorted her with their wild cries.

Phileas and his companions followed the chanting crowd.
They came to the edge of the river and stopped in full
view of the funeral pyre. Already the victim was stretched
out near her husband's corpse, still and quiet, seemingly
unconscious, lost in a drug-induced sleep.

The priests were coming down from the pyre. A torch
was brought. The wood at the foot of the pile took fire.
Phileas gave a little cry, and took a step forward, but was

seized and held back. He turned towards the pyre, then stood, rooted to the ground—

The whole scene had suddenly changed. On top of the funeral pile, the old Rajah had stood upright, like a phantom. He bent and took the young woman in his arms, and descended from the pile in the midst of clouds of smoke, which gave him a ghostly appearance.

A great wail passed over the crowd, who pressed their faces to the ground, moaning, not daring to lift their eyes to look at such a wondrous thing!

Before the startled gaze of Phileas and his companions, the old Rajah came down to the foot of the pile, and began to walk towards them, his burden in his arms. They stood, stupefied, until he was only a few paces from them.

He spoke.

"Help me to carry her," he said, "and let us get away!"

The voice was that of Passepartout! It was he who had slipped up to the pile in the darkness, and in the midst of the thick smoke! It was Passepartout, who had escaped in the midst of the general fright.

They slipped away into the woods and clambered on to the kneeling elephant. The Parsee brought him to his feet, and set him going at a rapid trot. There were shouts and cries behind them, telling them that the trick had been discovered. The guards rushed after them, shooting wildly, but they could not match the pace of the eager elephant.

In a few moments, they were out of range of bullets, and went, swaying and plunging, along the forest track.

Chapter Nine

The Trial

It was broad daylight when the Parsee brought the elephant to a stop an hour later.

Sir Francis grasped Passepartout's hand; his master said to him, "Well done!" which in that gentleman's mouth was high praise, indeed. As for the young woman, Aouda, she knew nothing of what had passed. Wrapped in travelling cloaks, she was still slumped, unconscious, in one of the howdahs.

Sir Francis remarked to Phileas that her troubles were not yet over. If she stayed in India, she would inevitably fall again into the hands of her executioners, who would seek to recapture her. She would only be safe, if she was taken out of the country.

After a bite of food, they set off once more, and, towards ten o'clock, they entered Allahabad and made their way to the station. The interrupted railway line started again here, and trains covered the distance to Calcutta in less than a day and a night. Phileas ought then to arrive in time to catch the steamer which left at noon on the next day, October 25th, for Hong Kong.

They laid Aouda on a bench in the waiting-room of the station, and Passepartout was sent off to buy her robes,

shawls, and slippers. By the time he returned, Aouda was beginning to stir, and look about her with most beautiful dark eyes. The train was about to leave. Between them, they helped her to it, and sat her in a car.

The Parsee was waiting—and so was the elephant. Mr. Fogg handed to the guide the agreed sum and then said: "Do you wish to own this elephant? If so, it is yours."

The Parsee's eyes sparkled. "You are giving me a fortune!" he cried.

"It is not enough for all that you have done for us," Phileas replied, and gravely shook the hand of his Indian friend.

Five minutes later the train was speeding towards Benares, eighty miles from Allahabad.

During this journey the young woman completely revived. Imagine her astonishment to find herself on this railway, in this compartment, in the midst of travellers quite unknown to her!

Sir Francis calmed her, and told her the whole story, and, when he had done, Aouda thanked her deliverers, but it was her beautiful eyes, rather than her lips, that told them of her gratitude. Then, her thoughts carrying her back to the scenes of the suttee, she shuddered, knowing that India still held many dangers for her. Guessing what was in her mind, Phileas offered to take her to Hong-Kong, where she could stay until this affair had died out. She accepted the offer gratefully. She had a relative who was one of the principal merchants of that city, and who would take good care of her.

The train reached Benares soon after noon. This was where Sir Francis had to leave them. He shook hands with Phileas and Passepartout; was kissed by Aouda, which made his face go very red; then they parted.

Leaving Benares, the railway followed the Valley of the Ganges. At seven a.m. they drew in to Calcutta. The Hong-Kong steamer did not weigh anchor until noon. Phileas had five hours before him. Twenty-three days after leaving London, he was neither behind nor ahead of time.

As they were moving towards the station exit, a policeman stepped in front of them.

"Mr. Phileas Fogg?" he asked.

"Yes."

"Is this man your servant?"

"Yes."

"You will both be so kind as to follow me."

Phileas showed no sign of surprise. Passepartout wanted to argue the matter, but Phileas made him a sign to obey.

"May the young lady come with us?" he asked.

"She may," replied the policeman.

He led them to a palkighari, a four-wheeled vehicle drawn by two horses. They started off. No one spoke during the twenty minutes' ride. They entered the European quarter, and stopped before a brick building. The policeman left them in a room with grated windows.

"At half-past eight," he said, "you will appear before Judge Obadiah."

At half-past eight the policeman reappeared, and led

them into a court-room. They were told to sit upon a bench in front of the seats reserved for the magistrate and his clerk. This magistrate, Judge Obadiah, entered almost immediately. He was a large, fat man. He took down a wig hung on a nail and hastily put it on his head.

"The first case," he said.

"Phileas Fogg?" asked the clerk.

"I am here," replied Phileas.

"Passepartout?"

"Present! "replied Passepartout.

A door was opened; three Hindu priests were led in. Passepartout gave a start. His eyes opened wide. He did a bit of tongue-clicking.

"Parbleu!" he said. "These are the ones who stole my shoes!"

The clerk read, in a loud voice, a charge against Mr. Fogg and his servant, who were accused of having violated a sacred place.

"And as a proof here are the desecrator's shoes," he added, putting a pair on his desk.

"My shoes!" cried Passepartout.

At this a gleam of triumph showed in the pale eyes of Detective Fix, who was seated, unnoticed, among the crowd of European and Indian spectators. It was, of course, the detective who had sought out the priests of Malebar Hill and promised them large damages, knowing very well that the British Government was most severe upon this kind of trespass. Because of the time that had been spent

in rescuing Aouda, Fix and the Hindus had reached Calcutta before Phileas and his servant, whom the authorities had been warned by telegraph to arrest as they got out of the train.

The judge had heard Passepartout's words. "The facts are admitted?" he asked.

"Admitted," replied Mr. Fogg coldly.

"Inasmuch," continued the judge, "as the English law intends to protect equally all the religions of the people of India, I sentence the man Passepartout to fifteen days' imprisonment and a fine of three hundred pounds! And," went on the judge," since the master should be held responsible for the acts of his servant, I sentence Phileas Fogg to eight days' imprisonment, and a fine of one hundred and fifty pounds. Call the next case!"

Fix smiled with satisfaction. Eight days! More than enough time for his warrant to arrive!

Passepartout was crushed. The sentence would ruin his master!

Mr. Fogg did not even knit his eyebrows. He rose and said: "I offer bail."

"It is your right," replied the judge. "The bail is fixed at one thousand pounds for each of you."

"I will pay it," said Phileas Fogg, to the horror of Mr. Fix.

And he took from the carpet-bag, which Passepartout carried, a bundle of bank-notes, which he placed on the clerk's desk.

"Very well," said the judge, "you are free under bail."

"Let us go, then," said Phileas.

"But they should at least return my shoes," cried Passepartout angrily.

They returned him his shoes.

"Parbleu! these cost a lot," he murmured; "more than a thousand pounds each! And they pinch my toes, too!"

Shaking his head in disapproval, he followed Mr. Fogg and Aouda from the building. Fix went after them to see what they would do.

Mr. Fogg and his friends took a carriage; Fix called another, which followed behind. Mr. Fogg's carriage went directly to one of the wharves and stopped there.

Half a mile out in the harbour the steam-ship *Rangoon* was anchored, her sailing flag hoisted to the top of the mast. Eleven o'clock struck. Mr. Fogg was one hour ahead. Fix, to his chagrin, saw him get out of the carriage, and embark in a boat with Aouda and Passepartout.

The detective snapped an order to his own driver, who turned the carriage and sped back along the wharf. Forty minutes later, having left instructions for the warrant to be forwarded to him at Hong-Kong, he succeeded in getting on board the *Rangoon* without being seen by Passepartout. All his hopes were now concentrated on Hong-Kong. That city was still British soil, but the last he would find on the road. Beyond China and Japan, America would offer Mr. Fogg a certain refuge. The arrest of the robber must be made in Hong-Kong!

Chapter Ten

The Opium-house

The *Rangoon* made excellent progress on her voyage to Hong-Kong. So, too, did the friendship between Aouda and Phileas Fogg. Her gratitude to Phileas shone at all times from her lovely eyes. For his part, he listened to her and talked with her, and treated her with the utmost politeness—but never let his face show the slightest emotion.

Aouda, at first, did not know what to make of him, but Passepartout explained to her a little of the eccentric character of his master. He told her of the wager that was taking him around the world, and she smiled and clapped her hands, and said what a fine thing it was to do.

Detective Fix, meanwhile, was keeping to his cabin, to avoid meeting Passepartout. He was puzzled by the presence of Aouda. Who was she? How had she become Fogg's companion? Had Mr. Fogg undertaken his journey across India with the aim of joining this charming young person?

The time had come to question Passepartout, he decided. He must know more of Mr. Fogg's intentions. He went on deck. Passepartout was already there, and the detective rushed towards him, exclaiming: "Good heavens! are you on board the *Rangoon,* too?"

"Monsieur Fix!" cried Passepartout, much surprised. "I left you at Bombay, and I meet you again on the route to Hong-Kong! Are you, too, making the tour of the world?"

"No, no," replied Fix. "I expect to stop at Hong-Kong—for a few days, at least. We would have met before, but I have not been well, and have rested in my cabin. Tell me, how is your master?"

"In perfect health, and as punctual as his diary! We are not one day behind! And, Monsieur Fix, we have a most charming lady with us, now."

"A young lady?" said the detective, pretending surprise. And Passepartout told him the whole story.

Passepartout was much struck by the chance which had once more put Fix on his master's route. There was a strange coincidence in it all. He was ready to bet that Fix would leave Hong-Kong on the same steamer as they. Why?

"Ahah! I have it," Passepartout said to himself. "He is a spy whom the gentlemen of the Reform Club have put upon my master's heels to make quite sure that he is, indeed, making the tour of the world. Parbleu! this is undignified! To have Mr. Fogg, honest gentleman that he is, tracked by a spy!"

He decided to say nothing of his suspicions to his master, fearing that he would be hurt by such mistrust. For the moment, he would just watch Mr. Fix very closely....

At four in the morning, on October 31st, the *Rangoon*, having gained a half-day on its timetable, put in at Singa-

pore to take in coal. Phileas Fogg noted this gain in the proper column, then went ashore with Aouda, and hired a carriage to make a tour of the island.

Fix followed them secretly, while Passepartout went into town and purchased a large quantity of mangoes.

After driving about the country for two hours, Phileas and Aouda returned into the town, and then to the ship, followed by the detective.

At eleven o'clock the *Rangoon* slipped her moorings and put out to sea to make her voyage of thirteen hundred miles to Hong-Kong. Phileas Fogg needed to cover this distance in six days, in order to catch at Hong-Kong a steamer that was leaving on November 6th for Yokohama.

As luck would have it, the weather, which had been fine, changed with the last quarter of the moon. The steamer made heavy going in a high wind and rough seas. It was estimated that she would be twenty hours behind time at Hong-Kong; more, perhaps, if the storm did not ease up.

Finally, the wind dropped; the sea became calmer. Land was signalled on the 6th of November at five a.m. They were a day late, and, of course, would have missed the Yokohama steamer.

At six o'clock the pilot came on board. Mr. Fogg was waiting for him, and asked if he knew when a vessel would leave for Japan.

"Tomorrow morning at high water," replied the pilot. "The *Carnatic* should have left yesterday, but needed to have a boiler repaired. She's not sailing until tomorrow."

Here was luck, indeed!

In an hour the *Rangoon* was at the wharf, and the passengers landed. Chance had once again favoured Phileas Fogg. He was twenty-four hours behind time, but the steamer which crosses the Pacific from Yokohama to San Francisco was a direct connection with the Hong-Kong boat, and the former would not leave before the latter arrived. They would be twenty-four hours late at Yokohama, but it would be easy to make them up on the long voyage across the Pacific.

Since the *Carnatic* would not leave until five the next morning, Mr. Fogg had sixteen hours to make some arrangement for Aouda. On landing from the ship, he offered his arm to the young woman, and led her to a rickshaw.

A room was found for Aouda at an hotel, and Phileas told her that he would go immediately to find her relative. Passepartout would stay with her until his return.

He came back with bad news. Her relative had left Hong-Kong two years before. Having made his fortune, he had gone to live in Europe—in Holland, it was believed.

Calmly he announced that Aouda must come to Europe with them. Sweeping aside all her protestations he sent Passepartout to book three cabins on board the *Carnatic*.

Passepartout sauntered down to the wharf from which the *Carnatic* would leave. There he came upon Fix, walking up and down, his face anxious and moody.

No warrant had arrived! It must still be running after him, and would reach him only if he stopped some days in

this city. Since this was the last British territory on the route, Mr. Fogg would escape him finally, if he could not find some way of detaining him.

"Well, Monsieur Fix, have you decided to come with us to America?" asked Passepartout jovially.

"Yes," replied Fix, between closed teeth.

"I thought you would!" cried Passepartout, shaking with laughter. "Come, then, and engage your berth."

They entered the ticket-office and booked their cabins. The clerk told them that the repairs to the *Carnatic* had been completed, and that the steamer would leave at eight that evening, and not the next morning.

"Excellent!" said Passepartout. "I must tell my master immediately."

At this moment Fix took an extreme step. He decided to tell Passepartout everything; to try to enlist his aid. When they left the office, he urged the Frenchman to come and drink a glass of wine with him. He had the time. Passepartout was persuaded.

They turned into a tavern on the quay; found themselves in a large room, at the back of which were couches, furnished with cushions. Upon these couches lay a number of sleepers.

Some thirty or so men, European and Chinese, were seated at small tables. Some were smoking long, red-clay pipes, stuffed with little balls of opium, mixed with essence of rose.

Passepartout looked about him with interest.

He understood that they had entered an opium smoking-house, a thing of which he had heard, but never seen before.

Fix called for a bottle of a strong wine. "This will do you no harm," he said, pouring Passepartout a large glass of the stuff.

They sat and talked, the detective all the time keeping Passepartout's glass topped up. The bottle was soon emptied. Passepartout rose, a little unsteadily, and said that he must go.

"Wait," said Fix. "There's plenty of time. I have something to say to you. It concerns your master and will, I assure you, be of great interest to you."

Intrigued, Passepartout sat down again. Fix called for another bottle of wine.

"What have you to say to me?" asked Passepartout, his speech now a little thick.

"You have guessed who I am?" asked Fix.

"Parbleu!" said Passepartout, smiling crookedly. "You are an agent of the members of the Reform Club, with a mission to interfere with my master's journey—"

"You are mistaken," said Fix coldly, refilling the Frenchman's glass. "I am a police detective."

"You—a detective?"

"Yes, here is my commission."

Taking a paper from his pocket-book, he showed Passepartout a commission signed by the Commissioner of the Central Police. Passepartout, too stunned to speak,

looked at Fix, then drained his glass at a gulp. Mr. Fix kindly re-filled it for him.

"Mr. Fogg's bet," he said, "is only a cover for other things. He has tricked you—"

"Why?" demanded Passepartout.

"Listen. On September 29th, fifty-five thousand pounds were stolen from the Bank of England. Now look at this description of the thief. Is it not that of your master?"

"Humbug!" cried Passepartout, striking the table with his fist. "My master is the most honest man in the world!"

"How do you know?" replied Fix. "You've only been with him a short time. Did he not leave in a hurry, without trunks, carrying with him a large sum in bank-notes? Do you wish to be arrested as his accomplice? I am waiting for a warrant for his arrest. You must help me keep him in Hong-Kong. I'll share with you the reward of two thousand pounds—"

"I? Help you? Never! I would never betray him, not for all the gold in the world—"

"You refuse?"

"I refuse!"

"Very well. Let's forget about it. We've always been friends, since that day in Suez. Have another drink and we will say no more on the subject."

"All right, let's have another drink."

Passepartout felt he needed it. His head was in a whirl. He wanted to drive away the suspicions that kept forcing their way into his mind.

On the table were a few pipes filled with opium. Fix slipped one into Passepartout's hand, who took it, lifted it to his lips, lighted it took a few puffs, and then slumped forward over the table, his head on his arms. Fix raised his head, lifted an eyelid, nodded in satisfaction, and let the Frenchman slump down again. Then he paid his bill, and walked out, leaving the unconscious Passepartout behind.

Chapter Eleven

The Japanese Acrobat

Mr Fogg, meanwhile, had gone shopping with Aouda, and then returned to his hotel to dine. When Aouda went to her room, he sat for the rest of the evening reading *The Times.*

The next morning they discovered that Passepartout had not returned to the hotel overnight. Mr. Fogg made no comment, but took his carpet-bag, called for Aouda, and set off in a carriage for the wharf. There he learned that the *Carnatic* had sailed the evening before. Though he had counted on finding at the same time his servant and the steamer, not a sign of disappointment showed upon his face.

A man who had been watching him closely now came up. It was Fix. "Pardon me," he said, "But I hoped to find your servant here."

"So did we," said Aouda, "for we have not seen him since yesterday. I wonder if he has sailed without us aboard the *Carnatic?*"

"Did you, then, expect to leave by that steamer?"

"Yes."

"So did I, but the Carnatic sailed twelve hours earlier than expected. We must now wait a week for another ship."

"Are there not other vessels in the port of Hong-Kong?" asked Phileas calmly, and, offering his arm to Aouda, he turned towards the docks.

Fix followed him as if a thread attached him to this man. There were plenty of vessels loading and unloading, but no ships ready for sea. Fix was beginning to hope again, when a sailor standing at the end of a pier spoke to Phileas.

"Looking for a boat, sir?" he asked, touching his cap.

"You have one ready to sail?" asked Mr. Fogg.

"Yes, sir—a pilot-boat, No. 43, the best in Hong-Kong. She'll give you eight or nine knots an hour. Do you want her for an excursion?"

"No, for a voyage. Will you take me to Yokohama? I've missed the sailing of the *Carnatic*, and I must be at Yokohama on the 14th, to catch the ship for San Francisco."

"Yokohama, sir? Sorry, that's impossible—"

"I'll pay you a hundred pounds a day, and a bonus of two hundred if I arrive in time."

The pilot looked at the sea, clearly struggling between his wish to earn the money and the fear of venturing so far.

"Look, sir," said the pilot, "there might be a way of helping you. I could take you to Shanghai, eight hundred miles from here. We shouldn't be any great distance from the coast and the currents run to the north—"

"But I want to catch the San Francisco steamer at Yokohama—"

"You will, sir. She doesn't start from Yokohama. She stops there, but her port of departure is Shanghai. She leaves there at seven in the evening, on the 11th. That gives us four clear days. Given the right weather, we can make it."

"It's a deal. You are master of this boat?"

"Yes, sir—John Bunsby, of the *Tankadere*."

"Here are two hundred pounds on account," said Phileas, paying from the carpet-bag. And then, turning to Fix: "Sir, if you wish to come with us—"

"You are very kind," said Fix awkwardly. "I was going to ask this favour of you."

"We shall be on board in half an hour."

While Fix, baffled and furious, followed the pilot to his boat, the other two went to the police-station, gave a description of Passepartout, and left a sum of money for him, if he should be found.

Returning to the pier they went on board the *Tankadere*. She was a sleek schooner of twenty tons. Her copper sheathing shone, and her deck was as white as ivory. She carried a crew of four, as well as her master, a lean and lively man in his forties.

The sails were hoisted; the *Tankadere* took the wind under her foresail and flew out into the sea, riding the waves like a gull.

By sunrise next morning, November the 8th, the little schooner had made more than a hundred miles. They moved on rapidly. John Bunsby had high hopes, and told Mr. Fogg several times that they would make it yet!

By evening of that day they had sailed two hundred and twenty miles. During the night, they entered the Formosa Strait. With daybreak the wind freshened, and the sea rose in long swells. Then the sky darkened.

"We're going to have a squall," said John Bunsby.

"Will it come from the north or the south?" asked Mr. Fogg simply.

"From the south. There's a storm coming up."

"Good," said Mr. Fogg. "It will blow us in the right direction."

John Bunsby had the sails reefed, and the hatches carefully secured. A single triangular sail was hoisted as a storm-jib, to hold the schooner's stern to the wind. They waited.

Towards eight o'clock they were struck by a storm of wind and rain. Under her little bit of sail, the *Tankadere* sped on towards the north. With nightfall, however, the storm grew wilder. It was impossible to sleep, and the passengers remained on deck, wrapped in oilskins. John Bunsby was uneasy.

"I think, sir," he said to Phileas at last, "we had best make for one of the ports of the coast."

"I only know one," said Mr. Fogg quietly.

"And that is?"

"Shanghai!"

John Bunsby blinked, stood a moment without speaking, then touched his cap, and said: "Ah, well, yes! Perhaps you're right." And the direction of the *Tankadere* was unwaveringly kept to the north.

It was truly a terrible night. Twice the little schooner was submerged, and everything would have been carried off the deck if the fastening of the ropes had given way. Aouda was worn out, but did not utter a word of complaint.

The storm was still raging when daylight came. However, the wind fell again into the south-east and the little craft drove on. From time to time, through a broken mist, they had glimpses of the coast, but not a ship in sight. The *Tankadere*, it seemed, was the only vessel keeping the sea.

During the afternoon, the wind and sea abated to some degree, and the passengers could eat a little and take some rest.

The night was fairly quiet. The sails were hoisted at low reef. The speed of the vessel was considerable. At dawn on the 11th, John Bunsby said that they were not one hundred miles from Shanghai.

One hundred miles—and only this day left to make the distance! The breeze slackened, and the sea fell away. The schooner was covered with canvas, and the sea foamed under her keel.

At noon they had forty-five miles to go, and six hours in which to do it! All felt their hearts beating impatiently—with the exception of Mr. Fogg, no doubt.

At six o'clock with the current in their favour, John Bunsby counted only twelve miles to Shanghai River, for the city itself is situated twelve miles above the mouth.

At seven o'clock they were still three miles off. John Bunsby swore. It seemed that his reward of two hundred

pounds was going to slip from his grasp. He looked at Mr. Fogg. Phileas' face told him nothing, although the sum of twenty thousand pounds was at stake at this moment.

At this moment, too, a long black funnel, crowned with a wreath of smoke, appeared on the horizon. It was the American steamer leaving at the regular hour.

"Curses on her!" cried John Bunsby.

"Signal her," said Phileas Fogg simply.

A signal-cannon stood on the forward deck of the *Tankadere*. It was loaded to the muzzle, but before it could be fired, Mr. Fogg said:

"Hoist your flag."

The flag was hoisted half-mast, a signal of distress. Perhaps the steamer, seeing it, would alter course to assist the little craft.

"Fire!" said Mr. Fogg.

The cannon boomed out. Every eye on board the *Tankadere* gazed longingly at the steamer. Still she kept her course. She had not seen.... Curse her! Curse—A cheer went up. The American captain, seeing a flag at half-mast, had turned his vessel towards the schooner.

A few minutes later, Phileas Fogg, paying for his passage at the price agreed upon, put in the pocket of John Bunsby five hundred and fifty pounds. Then he, Aouda, and Fix ascended to the deck of the steamer, which immediately set course for Yokohama, where it arrived on time, on the morning of November 14th.

Phileas Fogg went at once with Aouda to the French and

English consular agents to see if there were any news of Passepartout. Nothing had been heard of him, and they despaired of finding him again.

Aouda was much upset and worried, and Phileas, seeking to take her mind off things, took her into a Japanese theatre, close to the waterfront, to watch the performance of a troupe of Japanese acrobats and jugglers. The performers were highly skilled, and Aouda was delighted with their tricks and antics. The highlight of their performance was an unusual balancing act, performed by a group called "The Long Noses". Each wore a long nose, made of bamboos, five or six feet long. A group stretched themselves on the floor, their noses turned towards the ceiling. A second group balanced themselves upon the noses of the first, a third formed a story above, and then a fourth, making a human pyramid. The audience clapped like mad, the orchestra crashed like so much thunder, when all at once the pyramid shook, one of the "Long Noses" of the base rolled aside and leaped to his feet, the rest lost balance, and the pyramid fell like a house of cards.

The "Long Nose" who had left his post cleared the footlights with a bound, scattered orchestra and instruments to all sides, and fell at the feet of two spectators in the front row, crying:

"Master! master! I've found you!"

The voice was that of Passepartout!

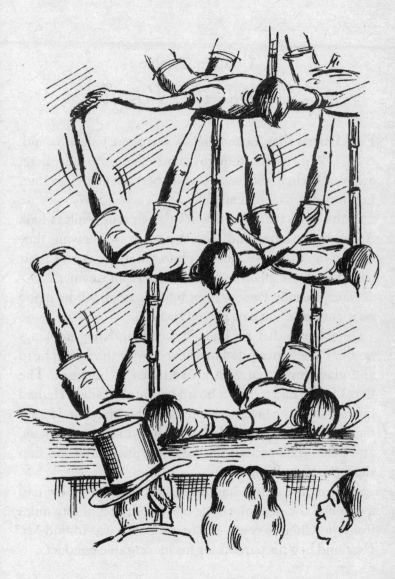

Chapter Twelve

Across the Pacific

Even Phileas Fogg looked slightly surprised, before he said, calmly, "Ah! Passepartout, my good fellow, so you are here, are you? Well, in that case, we had best not lose you again. Let us hurry to the steamer."

By this time the theatre was in an uproar. Phileas took Aouda by the hand, and, with Passepartout following, they fled to the main exit, and out into the street. A half hour later, they were all on board the American steamer.

Shame-facedly Passepartout told his story, but he made no mention of the part played by Fix.

Three hours after Fix had left the Hong-Kong smoking-house, Passepartout had awakened, with throbbing head and glassy eyes, but with a fixed idea in his head. The *Carnatic*! He had to be on board before she sailed! He had lurched from the tavern, staggered to the wharf, and found the ship ready to leave. He had rushed up the gang-plank, and fallen unconscious on the deck, just before the ship slipped her moorings.

Some of the sailors had taken him to a cabin. He had awakened the next morning, one hundred and fifty miles from the Chinese coast. His first thought was to find Mr. Fogg and beg his pardon for his inexcusable conduct.

He had gone to the purser and asked which cabin Mr. Fogg occupied. The purser replied that three cabins had been booked for a passenger of that name, but that he had not come on board when the ship sailed.

Passepartout was thunder-struck. But suddenly he remembered that the hour for the ship's departure had been advanced; that he had had to warn his master, and had failed to do so! It was his fault, then, if Mr. Fogg and Aouda had missed this steamer!

His fault, yes, but still more that of the traitor who, to separate him from his master, had made him drunk! At last he understood the detective's manoeuvre.

Now, here was he, Passepartout, on the road to Japan. He was certain of arriving there, but how was he to get away? His pocket was empty.

On the morning of the 13th the *Carnatic* entered the port of Yokohama. Passepartout went ashore and wandered the streets of the city. He could have asked for the help of the French consular agent, but hated to tell his story, and wished to exhaust all other chances first.

Then he had come across the Japanese theatre. When younger he had worked with a circus, and it had struck him that he might find employment. He had gone into the theatre and found the manager of the troupe. As luck would have it, an extra man was needed. Passepartout had been taken on as a "Long Nose"; with what results we already know....

Mr. Fogg listened coldly to this story, and made no

comment, but gave his servant money to buy more clothing on board. Very shortly, Passepartout was once again the dapper French man-servant.

The ship they were on was the *General Grant*. She was rigged as a three-masted schooner, and had a large surface of sails to aid her steam power. By making twelve knots she would need only twenty-one days to cross the Pacific. There was good reason, then, for Phileas to believe that, if he landed at San Francisco on December 2nd, he would be in New York on the 11th, and in London on the 20th, gaining some hours on the fatal date of December 21st.

All went well on the Pacific crossing. Nine days after leaving Yokohama, Phileas had covered half the distance of his round-the-world journey. On this day it happened that Passepartout made a joyful discovery. He had insisted on keeping his watch at London time, and had paid no regard to the time kept by the various countries through which he had travelled. Now this day, although he had not touched his watch, it agreed with the ship's chronometers.

"Ahah!" he cried triumphantly, "so the sun has decided to regulate itself by my watch!"

If, in fact, the face of his watch had been divided into twenty-four hours, then its hands, when it was nine in the morning on the ship, would have shown nine o'clock in the evening—a time-difference equal to that which exists between London and the one hundred and eightieth meridian.

Meanwhile Fix was still on their trail. In Yokohama he

had finally found the warrant of arrest at the English Consul's office. Running after him from Bombay, it was already forty days old—and useless, for Mr. Fogg had left the English possessions behind him.

"Very well," said Fix, "if it is no good here, it will be in England. I will follow him there, if that's where he's going!"

He booked a passage on the *General Grant*, hid himself in his cabin, and, thanks to the number of passengers, counted on not being seen by his enemy.

Two days before the ship was due to dock, however, he took a walk on the forward deck and found himself face to face with Passepartout.

"Parbleu!" said Passepartout, raising his fist, "it will give me much pleasure to thrash you!"

Without any explanation Passepartout caught him by the throat, and greatly to the delight of certain Americans who bet on the result, he administered a considerable thrashing to the detective and demonstrated the undoubted superiority of the French system of boxing.

"No more!" cried the detective. "I am no longer trying to delay Mr. Fogg. I wish to help him."

"Ah," said Passepartout, lowering his fist, "you have at last realized that he is an honest man!"

"Perhaps," said Fix hastily. "At any rate, I will do everything I can to help him reach England. There, at least, you will learn for certain whether or not you are in the service of a criminal. Well, are we to be friends?"

"Friends, no!" replied Passepartout firmly. "Allies, if you so please to a certain extent, for at the first sign of double-dealing or treason, I will have no hesitation whatsoever in wringing your neck."

"Agreed," said Fix calmly.

And with that, he stalked off.

Two days after, on December 3rd, the *General Grant* entered the Bay of the Golden Gate.

Mr. Fogg had reached San Francisco without losing or gaining a single day.

Chapter Thirteen

Sioux!

It was seven in the morning when Phileas, Aouda, and Passepartout set foot on American soil. Phileas immediately checked the hour at which the first train left for New York. Six in the evening. He had, then, a whole day to spare in the Californian capital. He ordered a carriage, they were taken to the International Hotel, and there booked rooms for the day.

When they had bathed and breakfasted, Phileas and Aouda left the hotel to go to the office of the English Consul. Before he left Passepartout asked his master if it would not be wise to buy a few Colt's revolvers, since he had heard that the Red Indians sometimes attacked and looted the trains. Mr. Fogg told him to act as he thought best.

When Phileas returned to the hotel, Passepartout was waiting for his master with half-a-dozen breech-loading revolvers. Phileas did no more than raise his eyebrows, and the revolvers were placed in the carpet-bag.

It was six in the evening when their train left San Francisco to make the seven-day journey to New York. Night had already fallen, cold and dreary, with an overcast sky. Fix had joined the others in their car, but they talked little. Passepartout sat near the detective, but did not speak to

him. He was, in fact, ready at the least suspicion to choke
the life out of his former friend!

In the morning, the train followed the windings of the
Sierra, clinging to the sides of the mountains, suspended
above precipices, and from time to time plunging into nar-
row gorges.

At three in the afternoon the train was brought to a halt
by a herd of ten or twelve thousand bison crossing the
tracks ahead. They could only wait, and darkness had come
down before the track was clear again. On they sped—
past the Great Salt Lake, through Wyoming Territory, on
over the Rockies, and down to the vast American plains.

When they came to Denver, the principal town of Colo-
rado, they had come thirteen hundred and eighty-two miles
from San Francisco in three days and nights. Four more
days and nights should see them in New York. Phileas was
still within his time if nothing interfered with the smooth
running of the train....

They had left North Platte behind them and were running over the plains of Nebraska when a bullet shattered
the glass of a window with a splintering crash. At once
there came a hail of shots; shouts and screams from the
passengers; wild and savage whoops outside.

A band of armed Sioux were galloping their ponies along-
side and firing as they rode. The passengers, nearly all
armed, replied with shots from their revolvers.

"We must defend ourselves!" cried Passepartout, and
handed a revolver to Phileas, to Fix, and even to Aouda.

Phileas knelt coolly by the broken window, knocked out some jagged ends of glass, took aim, and fired. An Indian fell headfirst off his racing pony, and turned head over heels in the grass.

Aouda, revolver in hand, crouched beside Phileas, firing through the broken panes whenever some savage presented himself.

The Sioux were on both sides of the train, screaming and yelling wildly. Some galloped in close to the moving cars and swung themselves from their ponies on to the rear platforms, drove in the doors, and fought hand to hand with the passengers. Others ran like enraged monkeys over the roofs.

Two of them had swung themselves on to the driving platform of the engine, where the driver and fireman lay stunned by blows from rifle-butts. A Sioux, wishing to stop the train, but not knowing how to use the handle of the regulator, had opened the steam valve instead of closing it, and the locomotive ran on at frightful speed.

The conductor lurched into the car where Phileas and his companions were, and shouted that the train must be stopped. Fort Kearney Station was two miles off. There was a military post there, but if the train swept past then the Sioux could not be beaten off.

Before he could be stopped, Passepartout had opened the rear door, gone out on to the platform, and succeeded in slipping under the car. Whilst the running fight continued, he made his way under the cars, clinging to the chains,

helping himself by the lever of the brakes and the edges of window-sashes, climbing from one car to another with mar-vellous agility, until he reached the front of the train.

There, clinging between the baggage car and the tender with one hand, he loosened the couplings, with the other. A sudden jolt of the engine made the yoking-bar jump out, and the detached train was left farther and farther behind, while the locomotive flew on with new speed.

The train rolled on for a minute or two, but finally dragged to a halt not one hundred paces from Kearney station. The soldiers of the fort were running towards the cars, firing as they came. The Sioux had turned their po-nies and were galloping off.

Scattered shots, then silence. Wearily the passengers swung down from the cars, and gathered on the platform of the station. Suddenly it was noticed that several passen-gers were missing—among them the courageous French-man whose brave act had saved them!

Chapter Fourteen
The Ice-yacht

Three passengers were missing. Had they been killed, or taken prisoner by the Sioux? As yet it could not be told.

There were a number of wounded, and they were carried to the fort for treatment. Aouda was unhurt; Phileas had not a scratch; Fix was safe and sound. But the gallant Passepartout was missing!

"I will find him dead or alive," Phileas told Aouda, though he knew that one day's delay would cause him to miss the steamer from New York.

The captain in charge of Fort Kearney was at the station, with about a hundred men. Phileas Fogg told him that he intended to go alone and look for the missing passengers. The captain was so impressed by Phileas' determined bravery that he sent thirty volunteers from among his men to help him in the search.

Fix wanted to go with them, but Phileas said, "You will do me a greater service, if you will stay with this young lady—in case anything should happen to me."

The detective's eyes dropped before the frank look that Phileas gave him. "I will remain," he said.

A horse and rifle were found for Phileas, and he rode off with the troop. It was then a few minutes past noon.

Aouda sat in the station waiting-room, thinking of Phileas Fogg, his generosity, his quiet courage. Phileas had become a hero in her eyes. Fix walked moodily up and down the platform.

At two in the afternoon, when snow had begun to fall in large flakes, a locomotive drew into the station from the east. It was the one which had been pulling the train, and which had gone off at such high speed, carrying the unconscious driver and fireman. The Sioux had soon given up the chase. After several miles, the fire had gone down for want of fuel, the steam had slackened, and the engine had come to a halt twenty miles beyond Fort Kearney.

When they came to, the driver and fireman realized what must have happened, and did not doubt that the train and passengers, left behind, were in distress. Coal and wood were thrown into the furnace, the fire started up again, the head of steam increased, and the engine returned running backwards to Kearney Station.

The passengers were overjoyed when they saw the locomotive put at the head of the train, and knew that they would be able to continue their journey.

The crew of the train were preparing to leave at once. Aouda begged the conductor to wait until Phileas and the others returned. He was kind but firm. Already the train was behind schedule. The next train would arrive on the following evening and they could continue their journey then.

Little did he know that day could cost twenty thousand pounds!

The engine whistled, the train started, and soon disappeared in the whirling flurries of snow. Aouda and the detective, Fix, remained at the station.

Some hours passed. The weather grew worse, the cold was bitter. Aouda went to the end of the platform and tried to see through the blizzard, listening to hear any sound. She saw nothing; heard nothing. She went in, chilled through, to return a few minutes later—again and again, and always in vain.

Night came. The little detachment had not returned. Aouda did not sleep at all. Her mind, filled with anguish, was wandering with Phileas on the prairie. Her imagination showed her a thousand dangers.

At dawn the captain called one of his lieutenants and ordered him to throw out a reconnaissance to the south. A moment later shots were heard. Was it a signal? The captain rushed from the fort and saw, half a mile off, a small band returning across the snow.

Phileas Fogg rode at the head, and near him Passepartout and the other two, rescued from the hands of the Sioux. There had been a fight ten miles south of Fort Kearney. Passepartout and his two companions were already struggling against their captors, when the soldiers arrived and rushed to their rescue.

Aouda took Phileas's hand, and pressed it in hers without being able to utter a word.

Passepartout was looking for the train.

"Where is the train, the passengers?" he cried.

"Gone," replied Fix.

"And when is the next one?" asked Phileas Fogg.

"Not until this evening."

"Ah!" said Phileas calmly.

They were twenty hours behind time.

"Look," said Fix, "if your journey hadn't been interrupted, you would have arrived in New York on the morning of the 11th."

"Yes, twelve hours before the departure of the steamer."

"Well, you are now twenty hours behind time. The difference between twenty and twelve is eight. You have eight hours to make up. Do you wish to try to do it?"

"On foot?" asked Mr. Fogg.

"No, on a sledge, a sledge with sails—an ice-yacht! A man offered to take me to Omaha in this way."

"Let us find him," said Phileas, "and make the attempt."

A few minutes later, Mr. Fogg was examining an unusual vehicle, a sort of frame laid on two long beams, a little raised in front, like the runners of a sledge, and on which five or six people could sit. In front of the frame was a high mast, to which an immense sail was attached; at the rear, a rudder for steering.

In a few moments the bargain had been struck, with the owner, Mr. Mudge. The wind was blowing strongly from the west; the snow had hardened, and Mudge was certain that he could take Mr. Fogg to Omaha in a few hours. From there, trains to New York were frequent, and it was not impossible to make up the time lost.

In less than an hour the ice-yacht was ready to start. The travellers took their places, wrapped in their travelling cloaks. The sail was hoisted, and, under the pressure of the wind, the ice-yacht slid over the hard snow at a speed of forty miles an hour.

They had two hundred miles to go. If the wind held, they could do it in five hours. If no accident happened, they ought to reach Omaha at one o'clock in the afternoon.

What a journey! The travellers, huddled up against each other, could not speak. The cold, increased by the speed, cut off their words. The ice-yacht glided as lightly over the surface of the plain as a ship over the sea.

"If nothing breaks, "said Mudge, "we shall arrive!"

There was no accident. At noon, Mudge told them that he was crossing the frozen course of the Platte River. Only twenty miles to go!

An hour later, he lowered the sail, and the ice-yacht glided to a halt before the station at Omaha. A through train was about to start. They had time to hurry into a car, and then the train was off.

The next day, the 10th, at four in the afternoon, they reached Chicago and passed immediately from one train into another. They were off again!

At nine thirty-five, on the evening of the 11th, their train stopped in the Jersey City Depot, near the pier of the Cunard line of steamers.

The *China*, bound for Liverpool, had left twenty minutes before!

Chapter Fifteen

Across the Atlantic

There was nothing to be done that night. Inquiries revealed that no other passenger-ship would sail for Liverpool for several days.

They spent the night in an hotel. Next morning, when Phileas arose at seven, he had nine days, thirteen hours, and forty-five minutes in which to reach London in the desired time.

He left the hotel; made his way to the docks, and looked for a ship about to sail. At last he saw one, moored a cable's length off-shore; a merchant-man, whose smoke-stack, pouring out clouds of smoke, seemed to show that she was about to leave.

Phileas hailed a boat, and was carried out to the *Henrietta,* an iron-hulled steamer, with upper parts of wood. Her captain was on deck; a man of fifty, tough, red-haired, and leathery.

Mr. Fogg introduced himself to the captain, whose name was Andrew Speedy. The *Henrietta* was due to sail in an hour's time for Bordeaux and, at first, the captain refused to take the party to Liverpool. When Phileas offered him two thousand dollars for each person, however, he changed his mind.

Phileas landed from the *Henrietta,* returned to the hotel, and brought back with him Aouda, Passepartout and the inseparable Fix, to whom he offered a passage. When the *Henrietta* was ready to sail, all four were on board.

At noon the next day, a man went up on to the bridge to take charge of the ship. It was not Captain Speedy! Not at all. It was Phileas Fogg. Captain Speedy was locked up in his cabin, and howling like a mad thing.

What had happened was very simple. Phileas Fogg wanted to go to Liverpool; the captain had gone back on their bargain and would not take him there. While he had been on board, Phileas had made such good use of his bank-notes that the crew, who were already on bad terms with the captain, now belonged to Phileas. The captain was shut up in his cabin, and the *Henrietta* was steering for Liverpool. Seeing Mr. Fogg at work on the bridge, it was clear that he had once been a sailor.

Passepartout was delighted by this latest exploit of his master. Fix was stunned. And Aouda said nothing. Passepartout, whose duty it was to take the captain his meals, did so with a Colt revolver in his hand.

On the 13th the wind shifted into the southeast and blew hard. Mr. Fogg had to reef his sails, and increase his steam. But the progress of the ship was slackened.

The 16th of December was the seventy-fifth day that had passed since leaving London. On this day, the engineer came up to the bridge and talked very earnestly with Mr. Fogg.

"Sir," he said, "since we left New York all our furnaces have been going. We had enough coal to go under a small head of steam from New York to Bordeaux, but we don't have enough for a full head of steam to Liverpool."

"I will think about it," replied Mr. Fogg. "For the moment, keep up your fires until all the coal is burned."

For two days more the ship sailed under full steam. On the morning of the 18th, however, the engineer informed Mr. Fogg that the coal would give out during the day.

"Don't let the fires go out," said Phileas. "And keep the valves charged."

He then told Passepartout to fetch Captain Speedy. A minute or two later the Captain dashed on to the bridge, his face purple with rage.

"Pirate!" he cried.

"I have sent for you, sir, to ask you to sell me your ship."

"No! by all the devils no!"

"I shall be obliged to burn her."

"Burn my ship!"

"At least her upper portions, for we are out of fuel."

"Burn my ship! A ship that is worth fifty thousand dollars!"

"Here are sixty thousand," replied Phileas, offering him a roll of bank-notes.

The captain looked at the roll. His ship was twenty years old. It might be quite a bargain!

"And the iron hull will be left to me?" asked the captain.

"The iron hull and the engine, sir. Is it a bargain?"

"It's a bargain!"

"Very well. Cut away all the wooden fittings, and fire the furnaces!"

On that day, the poop-deck, the cabins, the bunks, and the furnishing all went to maintain the steam at full pressure. The next day, the 19th of December, they burned the masts, the rafts, and the spars. On the 20th, the railings and the greater part of the deck were eaten up by the furnaces. The *Henrietta* was now a vessel cut down like a pontoon.

But on this day they sighted the Irish coast. At ten in the evening they were passing Queenstown. Phileas Fogg had twenty-four hours to reach London—and nearly all the wood had been used up!

"We will put into Queenstown," said Phileas calmly.

Queenstown is a port at which the transatlantic steamers deposit their mail-bags, which are carried to Dublin by express trains. From Dublin, they are taken to Liverpool by very swift vessels, so gaining twelve hours over the fastest ocean liner. Phileas meant to gain those twelve hours for himself.

Towards one in the morning, the *Henrietta* entered Queenstown harbour on the flood tide. Phileas Fogg left Captain Speedy on the levelled hulk of his vessel, still worth half of what he had sold it for.

With Aouda, Passepartout, and Fix, he jumped into a train at half-past one, reached Dublin at break of day, and immediately boarded a fast steamer for Liverpool.

At twenty minutes before noon, on the 21st December, Phileas Fogg finally landed on the quay at Liverpool. He was now only six hours from London.

But at this moment Fix approached him, put a hand on his shoulder, and, showing his warrant, said, "Phileas Fogg, I am a police officer. I arrest you in the name of the Queen!"

Chapter Sixteen

A Question of Time

Phileas Fogg was a prisoner. He had been shut up in the Custom House in Liverpool, and was to pass the night there, awaiting his transfer to London.

At the moment of his master's arrest, Passepartout had tried to rush upon the detective. Three policemen held him back. Aouda could not understand what it all meant. Passepartout explained to her that Mr. Fogg, this courageous gentleman to whom she owed her life, had been arrested as a robber. The tears flowed from her eyes. The two of them remained under the porch of the Custom House. Neither of them would leave the place. They would not desert Mr. Fogg.

As for that gentleman, his arrest would finally ruin him. Having arrived at Liverpool twenty minutes before noon, he had until a quarter to nine in the evening to appear at the Reform Club; he had, that is, nine hours and five minutes, and he only needed six hours to reach London.

He sat on a hard bench in the Custom House, his watch on the table before him, watching the movement of the hands. He waited. The Custom House clock struck one. He saw that his watch was two hours fast by this clock. Two hours! If he could jump into an express train at this

moment he could still arrive in London on time. A light frown passed over his forehead.

At thirty-three minutes past two there was a noise outside; footsteps, the opening of doors. He heard the voices of Passepartout and Aouda. The door was thrown open, and Fix, Aouda, Passepartout all rushed to him.

Fix was out of breath, his hair all disordered. He could hardly speak. "Sir," he stammered, "pardon—an unfortunate resemblance—robber arrested three days ago—you are—free."

Phileas rose to his feet. He looked the detective full in the face, then swung his fist and landed Fix a blow that stretched him flat.

"Well hit!" cried Passepartout.

Fix said nothing. He was unconscious. The other three rushed from the Custom House, jumped into a carriage, and in a few minutes reached the station. It was then forty minutes past two. The London express had left thirty-five minutes before.

Phileas Fogg then ordered a special train. It could not leave, however, before three o'clock. As luck would have it, there were delays along the line, and when their train pulled in to London all the clocks of the station showed that the time was ten minutes to nine.

Phileas Fogg, having been all the way around the world, had arrived five minutes behind time!

He had lost his bet!

Phileas was ruined. There was very little left of the twenty

thousand pounds he had taken away with him. He had only another twenty thousand deposited at Baring Brothers, and this he owed to his colleagues at the Reform Club. His wager had ruined him entirely. Well, he knew what remained for him to do.

Passepartout, knowing his master's state of mind, watched him closely, fearing that he might decide to take his life. But first the good fellow went to his own room and turned off the gas-burner which had been burning for eighty days at his expense!

The night passed. Mr. Fogg retired to his room, but did he sleep? Passepartout watched, like a dog, at his master's door.

The next morning Mr. Fogg rang for him and ordered him to prepare Aouda's breakfast. For himself, he said, he would be satisfied with a cup of tea and a slice of toast. Passepartout must ask Aouda to excuse him from breakfast and dinner, for all his time would be devoted to arranging his affairs. He would not come down. He would only ask to have a few minutes' talk with Aouda in the evening.

So, during this day, Phileas Fogg did not go to his Club when Big Ben struck half-past eleven. He had no need. It was not even necessary that he should go to his banker's to draw this sum of twenty thousand pounds. His opponents already had his cheque. He had nothing to take him out, and he did not go out. He remained in his room.

About half-past seven, he sent to ask Aouda if she cared

to spare him a few minutes, and, when she came to him, he sat opposite her, his face quite calm.

"Will you pardon me for having brought you to England?" he asked. "When I first suggested it, I was a fairly rich man, and counted on having money to place at your disposal. Now, I am ruined."

"Mr. Fogg," replied the young woman, "will you pardon me for having followed you, and who knows?—for having perhaps assisted in your ruin by delaying you? What will become of you now?"

"For myself, I need little," replied Phileas.

"Your friends—"

"I have no friends."

"Your relatives—"

"I have no relatives any more."

"Have you no one to share your troubles?" asked Aouda, and she rose and held out her hands to him. "Mr. Fogg, do you wish to have a relative and a friend? Will you not have me for your wife?"

Mr. Fogg, at this, rose in his turn. His lips trembled. His eyes opened wide. Then his arms went round her.

"I love you. I love you, and have loved you for many days!"

"Ah!" said Aouda.

Some minutes later, Mr. Fogg rang for Passepartout. He came at once. Mr. Fogg was holding Aouda's hand. Passepartout understood, and beamed his delight.

Mr. Fogg asked him if it would be too late to notify the

Rev. Samuel Wilson, of Marylebone Parish. Passepartout gave his most genial smile.

"Never too late," he said.

It was then five minutes after eight.

"It will be for tomorrow, Monday?" he said.

"For tomorrow, Monday?" asked Mr. Fogg, looking at Aouda.

"For tomorrow, Monday!" replied Aouda.

Passepartout went off, running as hard as he could.

It is time to tell here what a change of opinion there had been in London when the newspapers told of the arrest in Edinburgh on December 17th, of the true robber of the Bank of England, a certain James Strand.

Until then, Phileas Fogg had been a criminal whom the police were pursuing; now he was once again a most honest gentleman, accomplishing mathematically his tour round the world.

What an excitement in the papers! Betting began again with new energy.

Phileas' colleagues, at the Reform Club, passed these three days after the arrest in some uneasiness. Would Phileas Fogg reappear at the stated time? Where was he at this moment? On the 17th, it was seventy-six days since he had started out, and there had been no news of him. Was he dead? Had he given up the effort? Was he still on his way? Would he reappear on Saturday, December 21st, at a quarter to nine, on the threshold of the saloon of the Reform Club?

All London, it seemed, wanted to know the answer to that. On Saturday evening there was a large crowd in Pall Mall, and overflowing into the neighbouring streets. The police had much difficulty in keeping the roads clear. Excitement grew with every passing second.

That evening, the five colleagues of Phileas Fogg were waiting in the grand saloon of the Reform Club. The clock showed twenty-five minutes after eight.

"Gentlemen," said Andrew Stuart, "only twenty minutes to go!"

"At what time did the last train get in from Liverpool?" asked Flanagan.

"Twenty-three minutes past seven," replied Gauthier. "The next one doesn't arrive until ten minutes after midnight."

"I think we may take it for granted that we have won our bet," said Stuart, happily rubbing his hands.

"Let us wait before deciding," said Samuel Fallentin. "He never arrives too late or too soon. He might appear here at the very last minute."

"Gentlemen, he has lost!" protested Stuart.

"You know that the *China*—the only steamer from New York to be of any use to him—arrived yesterday. Here is the passenger-list, published by the *Shipping Gazette*. The name of Phileas Fogg is not on it. I think it clear enough that he will not arrive in time. Tomorrow will be too late!"

"Oh, let's forget the matter for a while," said Flanagan. "Come, gentlemen, a game of whist."

They seated themselves at a card table, and tried to play. Their eyes kept going to the clock, however; their hearts beat a little more rapidly as the seconds ticked away.

The clock showed twenty minutes to nine.

"Five minutes yet," said Stuart.

They took up their cards again, but their eyes were fixed upon the clock.

"Seventeen minutes to nine," said Thomas Flanagan, dealing the cards.

They tried to concentrate on their game. The saloon was quiet, but outside they could hear the hubbub of the crowd. The clock ticked loudly, and each could count the seconds as they passed.

"One minute to go, "said John Sullivan, in a voice which shook a very little.

One more minute and the bet would be won. The cards lay forgotten. They were counting the seconds!

At the fortieth second, nothing. At the fiftieth still nothing!

At the fifty-fifth, there was a roaring like that of thunder outside.

The players rose.

At the fifty-seventh second, the door of the saloon opened, and Phileas Fogg appeared, followed by an excited crowd, who had forced an entry into the Club, and in his calm voice he said:

"Gentlemen, here I am!"

Yes! Phileas Fogg in person.

It will be remembered that, at five minutes past eight in the evening, some twenty-three hours after his arrival in London, Phileas had sent Passepartout to inform the Rev. Samuel Wilson of a marriage which was to take place the next day.

The Rev. Wilson was not at home, but expected back at any moment. Passepartout waited. At precisely thirty-five minutes past eight, he might have been seen running from the clergyman's house, his eyes wild, his hair disordered, upsetting passers-by, rushing along the pavements like a water-spout.

In three minutes exactly he was back at Mr. Fogg's house, and fell, breathless, into his master's room. He could not speak.

"What is the matter?" asked Mr. Fogg.

"M-m-marriage," stammered Passepartout, "i-i-im-im-possible—t-t-t-t-to-morrow!"

"What! Why?"

"T-t-t-to-morrow is *Sunday!*"

"Monday," replied Mr. Fogg.

"No—today—Saturday. You have made a mistake of one day. We arrived twenty-four hours ahead of time—but there are only ten minutes left!"

Phileas gave a cry, clapped a hand to his head, then tore from the house, jumped into a cab, promised a hundred pounds to the driver, and, after running over two dogs and running into five carriages, arrived at the Reform Club.

The clock showed a quarter to nine when he stepped

into the grand saloon. He had won his bet of twenty thousand pounds!

And now, how could so exact a man have made the mistake of a day? It is very simple. He had, without suspecting it, gained a day on his journey, because he had made his tour of the world going to the *east;* that is, towards the sun, and consequently the days became as many times four minutes less for him, as he crossed degrees in that direction. There are three hundred and sixty degrees in the earth's circumference, and this figure, multiplied by four minutes, gives twenty-four hours. In other words, while Phileas, travelling towards the east, saw the sun pass the meridian *eighty* times, his colleagues in London saw it pass only *seventy-nine* times. Therefore, on this very day, which was Saturday, and not Sunday as Mr. Fogg thought, his friends were waiting for him at the Reform Club. And Passepartout's watch, which had always kept London time, would have shown this, if it had shown days as well as the minutes and hours!

Phileas Fogg, then, had won the twenty thousand pounds. Since, however, his journey had cost him nineteen thousand, his reward was small. However, he had sought no more than to gain the victory and not to make money. Even the remaining thousand pounds he divided between Passepartout and the unfortunate Fix, against whom he could not cherish a grudge. Only, for the sake of exactness, he kept back from his servant the cost of the gas burned during their voyage round the world.

The marriage of Mr. Fogg and Aouda took place forty-eight hours later. Passepartout, superb, resplendent, beaming, was present as a witness.

Early next morning, he knocked noisily at his master's door. The door opened, and Phileas looked out.

"What is the matter, Passepartout?"

"Sir, I have just found out that we could make the tour of the world in seventy-eight days."

"Doubtless," replied Mr. Fogg, "by not crossing India. But if I had not crossed India, Aouda would not be my wife, and—"

And Mr. Fogg quietly shut the door.

Illustrated Chosen Classics
—————— Retold ——————

Titles available in this series:

PETER HADDOCK PUBLISHING